A Beach Day For Hannah

Photos & Story by Linda Petrie Bunch

Printed in the United States of America
Book Club Productions / Mountain Dog Books

**To order books visit MountainDogBooks.com
or write to hannah@mountaindogbooks.com.**

**Need books for a fundraiser?
Contact Hannah**

**Hannah is a Woofer & a Tweeter.
Follow her Dog Blog &
make Friends with her on Facebook!**

Petrie Bunch, Linda.
A beach day for Hannah / photos & story by Linda
Petrie Bunch.
p. cm. -- (Mountain dog books ; 2)
SUMMARY: In this rhyming story, Hannah, a Bernese
mountain dog, frolics on the beach, swimming,
bird-watching, building sand castles, surfing and
sailing in the sun.
Audience: Ages 1-10.
LCCN 2012902354
ISBN 978-0-9777781-9-5

1. Bernese mountain dog--Juvenile fiction.
2. Beaches--Juvenile fiction. [1. Bernese mountain dog--
Fiction. 2. Dogs--Fiction. 3. Beaches--Fiction.
4. Stories in rhyme.] I. Title. II. Series: Petrie
Bunch, Linda. Mountain dog books ; 2.

PZ8.3.P456Bea 2012   [E]
              QBI12-600046

Hannah the mountain dog
looked down at the beach.

The sand and the ocean
were just in her reach.

She bounced down a path,
the wind in her hair,

and took a long look
at the birds in the air.

The curious pup
climbed up on a rock,
but she didn't know
she was in for a shock!

She took a big leap
and dove into the sea,
with ears and paws flying,
how cold could it be?

Hannah made a big splash,
then swam a dog paddle.
The water was chilly.
It made her teeth rattle!

Out of the water,
shaking and soggy,
she licked off her lips -
a wet salty doggy!

Hannah wrapped herself up
in a bright colored towel,
then got an idea
and let out a howl.

She started to dig
with a shovel and pail,
and ran in a circle
wagging her tail.

A tiny blue bucket
got stuck on her nose.
She danced and she wiggled
from her head to her toes.

Using her beach toys and working alone, she built a dog castle shaped into a bone.

Hannah hid in a fort
that she made from bent sticks.
Gathering driftwood
was one of her tricks!

A boy with a board
had on a black suit,
that covered him up
from his head to his boot.

She swam through the water,
jumped on a surfboard.
She was riding big waves,
a thrilling reward!

Hannah got tired.
It was time for a snooze.
She dreamed of a hammock
and imagined a cruise.

She woke in a daze
and gazed down the shore.
Then noticed some boats
and ran to explore.

Hannah found a small ship
with sails flying high.
She climbed on the deck
and barked a "good bye!"

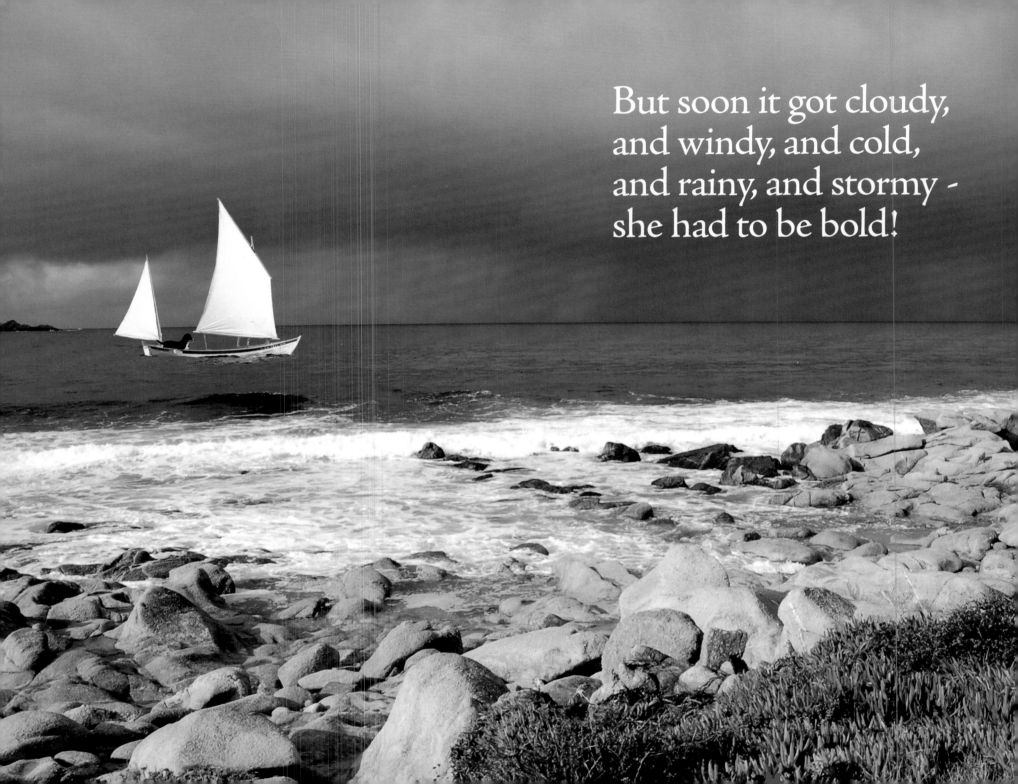

But soon it got cloudy,
and windy, and cold,
and rainy, and stormy -
she had to be bold!

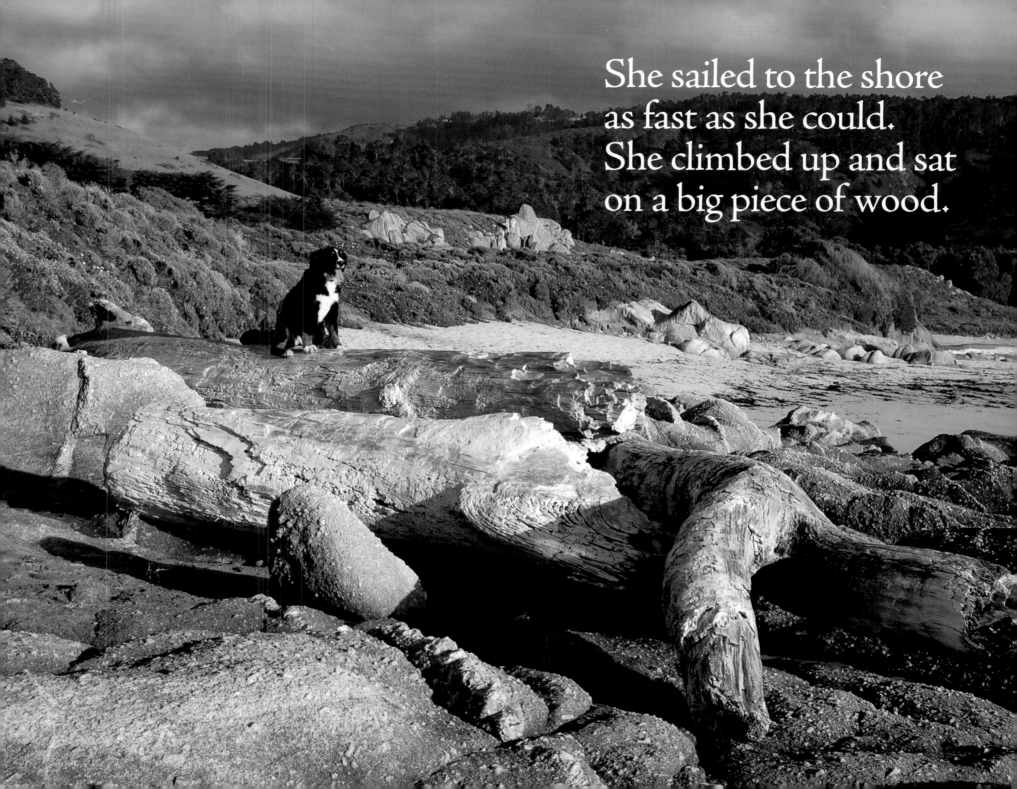

She sailed to the shore
as fast as she could.
She climbed up and sat
on a big piece of wood.

After the shower
Hannah let out a sigh.
A rainbow appeared
right out of the sky!

Down to the water
at the end of the day,
the ocean was quiet.
The birds flew away.

In silence she watched
the bright setting sun.
Hannah's day at the beach
had been lots of fun!